BORN TO DECEIVE

By

Isabella McKenzie

Born To Deceive

Printed by Ingram

ISBN: 978-1-66641-168-3

CONTENTS

ABOUT THE AUTHOR

Isabella McKenzie is a 15-year-old student living in the beautiful countryside of Surrey with her parents and younger sister. She balances her love of sports—league and adult's netball, volleyball, and kayaking—with a deep affection for English literature.

Her fascination with psychological thrillers and crime fiction has inspired her to take on the ambitious challenge of writing her first crime novel before sitting her GCSEs. Her determination to push creative boundaries shines through in her work, and she hopes her journey will encourage fellow teenage writers to embrace their own ideas and pursue their passions without fear.

For my friends and family,

I couldn't do any of this without you

BORN TO DECEIVE

CHAPTER 1
PRISON

Prison.

It wasn't just a prison literally, but a prison of my mind. I couldn't think freely. I couldn't speak freely. I was walking on eggshells, always watching who I looked at, the way I stared, or the amount of food I chose to eat. My life wasn't my own anymore.

At fourteen years old, I stood on an ice-cold concrete floor, a bitter wind swirling around me. My hands shook uncontrollably, and my heart constantly pounded out of my chest. I never understood what it felt like to see your life flash before your eyes, but I understood now. I could feel the blood gushing through the vessels in my head. It felt like a relentless monster, pulling and tearing at my brain. Every word I heard was like a violent jolt of unbearable pain, ripping at my skull from the inside out. This twisted knot of agony meant I could no longer think straight. I felt like I was going insane, and the only escape was the sweet release of unconsciousness.

I felt every eye in the dark, musty room on me, staring at me like an object, a science experiment, a monster that couldn't be explained. I hated it. I stared down at the unnerving ground, hoping for a warm breeze of comfort, but was greeted with another shout or stare. In a room with only thirty people, it felt like the world was staring at me, scrutinising me from the tip of my head to my shivering feet, pretending they knew what I had been through and what I had seen.

I knew I would never forget this: the constant paranoia of never knowing what people were saying, and the sight of my own face on the black screen that had held my sanity while I was mentally tortured for anything that would support my arrest. I was fourteen. Fourteen, and sitting in a dark room staring at the ceiling while I was surrounded by three men who only cared about making the arrest for something they knew I was not capable of.

The constant ringing in my head wouldn't leave, and even when the room was silent, I heard everything—every breath and thought, as loud as a scream. I couldn't help but notice that every member in this room had been here before, except me. They all had a sense of familiarity, but for me, I was petrified. Not knowing when I would see my family again constantly terrified me. My throat felt suffocated, the pungent smell overwhelmed my nostrils, and my bloodshot eyes began to flood like streams.

"No, no, no", I was screaming at myself. I swore I wasn't going to show any sign of weakness in this hell of a prison. The walls were falling apart with exposed brick and blood smeared as traces of former inmates.

I never thought I would be able to say I had been to prison, but that was before everything changed, before that night. The night when I woke up covered in blood with no recollection of the night before.

I had just barely finished year nine, and now I found myself in a damp room covered in years of dirt and grime. The only source of light came through a barricaded window, high up on one wall, covered by rough grey stone and engraved with the tally of days another inmate had been here.

To calm my anxiety and nausea, I decided to count the tally to quiet my mind, but I counted for hours on end and eventually landed at 2,758—just under eight years of hell. Counting didn't calm my mind but rather horrified it. I was only reminded that I was grouped with those people—murderers, rapists, horrible monsters—and they thought I was one of them. Me.

All around me, I could hear shouting, swearing, and constant fights. I was petrified. Every bone in my body jumped even when someone was pushed against a wall.

It was only then I realised how terrified I truly was. It had been less than a couple of days, and I would already give up anything to be free again.

I had one minuscule pea of hope that a date, a minute of security footage, a neighbour—something, anything—that could clear my name would come in. It already felt like decades since I had felt the warm sun glisten across my cheek and heard my mother tell me to clean my room or do my homework. I realised how much I missed that now. As I bowed my head to reflect on what had gotten me caught up in this mess, I heard a loud shout and cry, "Zandra! Zandra, where are you?" I could hear the pain in her voice and the grief in her wails. She ran straight up to the four walls that had kept me away from her motherly soul for what seemed like years. I lifted my head with everything I had left in me to see my mother's beautiful blue eyes. They contained a soft glow that felt like home. I gazed at her with wide eyes full of love and relief, and she gazed back as if she could see into the depths of my soul. I knew immediately I would cherish this moment for the rest of my life.

My heart was racing. My palms were dripping with sweat. I felt my heart lift as I took the first breath of clean air, but I couldn't savour it. Not yet. My heart skipped a beat as I watched the doors open, and I was able to look out with no one watching, judging, or standing behind me to make sure I didn't try to run. I tried so hard to enjoy it, but I knew this wasn't over yet. I knew I had to come back tomorrow for more questioning and that I would be stuck in the same four walls that drove me insane.

A small smile danced across my face when I laid eyes on the same black Honda I had known my entire life. I couldn't help but feel a sense of familiarity and comfort wash over me as the car neared the end of the journey. It felt like I was closer and closer to home. I took a deep sigh as I stared out the window, trying to act as normal as possible, but I knew it wasn't over when we turned a sharp corner and there seemed to be floods of people all screaming and shouting for me. News presenters, neighbours, journalists, and even just ordinary people. I quickly bent over and hid below the car window, holding my hands low to avoid showing any proof of my presence. As quickly as my smile had appeared, it disappeared, and the weight on my chest returned.

In that hellish place, I couldn't get my mind off my birth mother. Prison was a place she knew better than she knew me, and that made me question everything—her love for me, her passion, her care.

The long car drive seemed to go on forever, but at least the people had gone. Soon, I was back on the same old country road I had known my whole life. I peered out of the musty car window to glance at the small front porch of the house that had always felt like home. When we finally arrived, I opened the car door without hesitation. I felt so free as the white pebbles beneath my feet rolled across the driveway in the wind. This was home, and it meant the world to me to be back. I ran inside, the warm smell of homemade food making me so happy, and I found myself enjoying the cosy space that could fit a family—my family. Except not my birth family.

No matter what I couldn't help but wonder about my birth mother, knowing that to her, prison was like a second home. She was a criminal mastermind, but of course, no one could ever know that because she was the only person who knew I was her daughter. I was born at a time she could not support me, so she gave me away, but even today, she still comes to see me every night, on the hour.

CHAPTER 2
YOUNG AND NAIVE

The fireplace was still burning, and the blankets were folded in Mum's own special way, which made me feel almost normal. However, whenever I went to the sofa to watch a movie, it was always interrupted by the endless abyss of my face and name on every channel. I couldn't wait for this to be over. Every time I sat down to take a breath and have a moment of calm, I was greeted with the same headline: "14-year-old murderer." It was never-ending, but every time it came up, Mum hugged me, and her warm touch made me feel so safe in her arms. I started to smile as things were sort of falling into place, despite the fact that my name and face always showed up between movie breaks.

My eyes soon began to tire, and my eyelids felt like weights over my sleep-ridden eyes. As my exhausted body fell onto the bed, which I hadn't seen in what felt like months, it looked so welcoming, it was almost surreal. My muscles had never felt so sore, and all I wanted to do was collapse onto my soft mattress and let out a deep sigh of relief. As I crawled under the covers, I could feel the weight of the day's stress and fatigue slowly lifting off my shoulders.

The softness of my pillows and the warmth of my blankets instantly provided a sense of comfort that I had been craving all day. My eyes started to slowly shut, and my body sank deeper into the mattress as I let out a long, contented breath. It was as if my body knew it could rest and allow all my worries to fade away into the dark background as I sank into a deep, peaceful sleep. Just as my body was finally able to surrender to the calmness and tranquillity of the night, I heard a quiet noise. Not a naturally quiet noise, but a noise that was quiet because it was supposed to be.

Some people say that women have a sixth sense and can feel even when they are being watched or when someone is in their presence. I believe I always had that sense. My heart started racing, and my senses became heightened. I tried to dismiss it from my mind and convince myself it was only my imagination, but the strong feeling persisted. As I lay there, trapped in a cold, childish body, I became more and more certain that someone was in the room with me. My skin prickled with fear, and I could feel my breaths becoming shorter and shallower. I could sense their eyes on me. I felt completely exposed and vulnerable. I knew it wasn't my birth mother—she was always a little late, and she never gave me this feeling. This was the feeling of danger.

My mind started racing with all sorts of terrifying scenarios. Who could it be? What did they want from me? My fear became so overwhelming that I felt completely paralyzed, unable to move or even speak. Every sound in the room became amplified, and I was acutely aware of every creak and rustle. I was on high alert, ready to defend myself from whatever had been lurking in the shadows.

Suddenly, I noticed, with tears in my eyes and my heart beating like a drum, that a mysterious shadow was emerging from behind my curtains—curtains that had once kept me safe but now offered an opportunity for fear. They had once been a source of comfort but had now become a tool for destruction.

It was a tall, broad figure. I now realised it was a man. I felt the blood coursing through my head faster than ever, and I became filled with both fear and rage. I gasped and sat completely still when I saw a masculine black shoe step out from behind my curtain. He was now approaching my bed, stumbling forward, swinging his arms blindly, swearing and shouting the names of people I guessed he hated. As I observed his behaviour, questioning if he was intoxicated or mentally ill, he suddenly lunged toward me.

His arms were outstretched, ready to claw at my throat. I screamed with all I had left and threw myself out of bed, fighting for my life. I collapsed to the ground, shaking and crying, as he towered over my weak form with a sharp blade clenched in his fist.

Never in my life had I given up, but in that moment, it was as if time stood still and my life was going to change forever. I stared up at his strong, tall body, which seemed to be crushing my organs. As he slowly lifted the sharpest blade I had ever seen, I knew it was over—that all my dreams would remain dreams forever. He stared into my red, stinging eyes filled with tears and placed the knife against me. I felt it violently press against my throat, and I started wailing and screaming. Then I stopped when I felt a stream of liquid trace down my chest. That's when I knew it was over.

Just before my lifeless eyes closed for the last time, I felt a warm drop of blood fall gently onto my forehead, and I heard a loud thud as this horrible monster fell to the ground beside me. My forever curious eyes fluttered open once more to glance up to see my mother, my birth mother, standing over his body. It was almost ironic, she chose to murder him and bring me his body over staying with her daughter during her last moments, my last moments, I couldn't say I was surprised. The last thing I heard was his empty heart stop beating. That's when I smiled.

I gasped for air, feeling as though my heart was being strangled. I didn't realise that was going to be my last breath.

CHAPTER 3
MY DAUGHTER

I'm three minutes later than yesterday. It was almost funny to me that I didn't feel remorse for the numerous deaths I had orchestrated, but when it came to my daughter, even a minute late reminded me why she deserved better than me. My regular routine kicked in: I'd have a letter written for her to let her know I was there and that I loved her, and I'd take a chance to glance at the face of my beautiful girl.

She was okay now; she had grown up in a good family, in a good area, with good people, and that was something I could never have offered her. She was adopted. My life was too involved with crime and debt to have raised the wonderful person she had become. It didn't seem right that just this morning, I had watched her on the news, getting out of jail for a crime I knew she didn't commit. The prison system is cruel; they never seem to catch the right ones, like me or the people I call my family, only the young girls who can't defend themselves in a court system, who are just looking to close a case.

It was time to go in now, so I crawled through the window, hoping to hear a "Hey, Mum" or "How are you?"

Instead, it was eerily was silent, and my heart dropped. I had that feeling— it settled deep in my gut, a knowing certainty that something was horribly wrong. I tiptoed closer to the bed, and there she was, lifeless. Her eyes were glazed over, and her stomach was becoming swollen. My heart raced, my blood ran cold, and I became a blind fit of anger, ready to unleash hell on anyone or anything that stood in my way. I had no choice;

I had to go.

My daughter's most vulnerable moment, and I had to leave her. I knew I would drown in the guilt it would inflict on me, but I had no other option. I was not going to go down for the murder of my daughter when the police or an ambulance arrived. I would not be able to prove I didn't do it, not with my criminal history. I had no choice. I kissed her on the forehead, closed my eyes, savouring my last moments with her, and left. However, as my lips brushed against her skin I felt it—just the faintest, most fragile breath on my neck. It was weak, almost imperceptible, but it was still very much there, in that moment I realised I had to find them and bring her justice. It was the best I could do for her, the least I could do for her.

I opened the window again in a blind rage and slammed it shut as I jumped down from the side of her home, only to see a man, tall and broad. It seemed like nothing to him that he was dressed in full black in the middle of the night, talking on the phone. I felt something in the air, a sense, a feeling that this was *Him*.

The man who had just ripped the love of my life away from me was casually talking on the phone after ending my daughter's life. His indifference made my blood boil, and I couldn't hold back. I wouldn't. I reached for my knife.

CHAPTER 4
DETECTIVE NANCY

I stared down at what was now the bloodiest murder scene I had ever witnessed. My name is Nancy Richmond, and I have been a Detective for as long as I can remember. I have seen everything—from bank robberies to kidnappings and body bags—but nothing like this. Every scene has usually been altered before the police arrive, whether it's a panicked witness or the bleaching of blood out of carpets and clothes to hide evidence, but in this case, it was a raw room. Blood was violently splattered across the traumatised walls, the carpet stained beyond measure, and the most powerful pungent odour of a decomposing body. However, none of the sounds, smells, or tastes in the rotting air could compare to her eyes bulging like marbles out of her young, bruised face, her gas-filled stomach, and the purple veins coursing along her arms.

Her hair was tangled and matted, but it didn't take away from the gaping tear in what once was the innocent neck of a girl—a daughter, a child. Her mouth showed pink as her own blood mingled with the cloudy, white froth that matched the whites of her eyes. She looked like hell unleashed on earth. The monster that committed this act of evil would never truly pay for the petrifying murder of this girl, who had once been full of dreams and goals and was now sitting still, her organs starting to digest themselves.

This was the most pivotal moment of my career, and I knew I would never forget it. My heart sank. It's always tough to see someone so young lose their life in such a brutal manner before it has even begun. As my eyes darted across the huge blood-ridden room, I searched frantically for anything that could bring justice to this poor girl and her terrified family. I noticed large black footprints that seemed to resemble the shape of a boot. I asked Chief Superintendent Reynolds to take a small sample of the jet-black, musty dirt that stained the carpet so I could conduct my own investigation into where the suspect had been before committing the murder.

Chief has always been my idol. Her diligence has closed thousands of cases, and she can handle even the toughest cases, like this one, without shedding a tear. She agreed but with caution and stared down at me as if I were not to be trusted. There was always a part of her that couldn't let anyone have the ability to tamper with evidence. Reluctantly, I slowly picked up a small piece of fabric near the victim's ice-cold, dismembered body and realised it was a unique piece with a distinctive black and white pattern of swirls and lines. Only then did I realise that I had seen it before.

I glanced over at the bodies and stared down at the large black boots on one of the victims—a male, who definitely would have been tall and muscular. That's when it clicked. These two people were nothing alike. One was a young girl, choosing her GCSEs and going to school while being convicted of a crime, we all suspected she didn't commit, now with her throat slit next to the dismembered remains of a gang member.

He was a tall man with a different family, a history of drug and alcohol abuse, and who had recently recovered from a car accident. This meant it was possibly a murder-suicide. As a result, this case was well thought out and calculated. Right now, I had a bigger problem—there was no murderer alive to arrest, and that meant no justice for her family.

My heart sank as I realised this case couldn't go any further.

As evidence, I placed the small piece of fabric and the DNA samples deep into my worn pocket. My mind was spinning, overwhelmed with possible motives, and then it crossed my mind that there's always a silver lining. I knew this would be my big break after my last disastrous case. A smile spread across my face as I realised this was my chance to prove everyone wrong and show them that the murder of my former partner Sophie had nothing to do with me. The stares in shops, the comments online, and the second looks at my CV would finally end. A chilling thrill coursed through my veins, as I realised fate had finally tipped in my favour.

A tear caressed my face as it slowly fell from my terrified, watering eye. I realised that this girl's life, lost in such a destructive and inhumane way, would elevate my career. My heart wept for her; I couldn't bear to look at her lifeless body any longer. Solemnly, I walked out of the room that now smelled of rot and decomposing bodies. As I stepped out of the crime scene, my heart pounded in my chest, a wild mix of adrenaline and fear racing through my veins.

The scene I had just witnessed was unlike anything I had encountered in my years as a Detective. The air was heavy with an ominous stillness, and the echoes of terror lingered in the depths of my mind. Every step I took away from that haunting room felt like a weight lifting off my shoulders, yet a part of me remained trapped within its dark embrace. The images played over and over in my mind, etching themselves into my memory, refusing to fade. The coldness of the room, the metallic scent of blood, and the eerie silence pierced my thoughts, sending a shiver down my spine.

CHAPTER 5
TRAUMA

My usually steady hands trembled with a mixture of anxiety and confusion. The magnitude of the crime scene had left an undeniable mark, forever altering my perception of the world. I had seen the true depths of human depravity—a terrifying glimpse into the abyss of evil. I decided to walk home early, but with every step, the faces of the victims haunted me, their lifeless eyes carved into my consciousness. The anguish and pain she must have endured in her final moments weighed heavily on my conscience. I couldn't help but question whether I had done enough, whether I had missed crucial details that could have altered the outcome.

Leaving the crime scene didn't bring relief as I had hoped. Instead, a thunderstorm of conflicting emotions consumed me. A sense of failure mingled with a burning determination to bring justice to her family, who had just lost their only daughter and witnessed a scene they would never be able to erase from their minds. The fear that had gripped me within those walls lingered, seeping into every pore of my being. I couldn't escape the feeling that darkness was lurking around every corner, ready to strike at any moment.

The world appeared different, tainted by the horrors I had witnessed, but a flicker of resilience ignited within me. I vowed to use the fear as fuel, to channel my unease into unwavering determination. The haunting crime scene had left a lasting impact, but I refused to be paralyzed by it. My steps may have been heavy, but my spirit remained unbroken. The journey ahead would be long and difficult, but I was committed to unravelling the truth, bringing justice to those who had suffered, and finding peace for myself as my heavy eyes slowly closed with relief.

I slowly opened my eyes, anxiety clinging to my body like a heavy shroud. It was morning, or at least it seemed like it. The room was dimly lit, casting long shadows across the worn-out furniture.

As my vision adjusted to the muted light, memories of the previous day flooded back, crashing against the fragile walls of my mind. That was when I realised this case had taken its toll on me. The murder of a young girl had struck deep within my core, leaving an indelible mark on my soul. Every waking moment was consumed by thoughts of her, her innocent face haunting my dreams. The weight of the unresolved crime had become an unrelenting burden on my shoulders.

As I sat up on the edge of the bed, my weary limbs protested, reminding me of the physical and emotional exhaustion I had endured. My mind, once sharp and focused, now felt cluttered, overrun with images and fragments of evidence. It was as if a jigsaw puzzle had exploded in my head, with pieces all from different puzzles, impossible to assemble.

I dragged myself to the bathroom, catching a glimpse of my haggard reflection in the mirror. Dark circles framed my bloodshot eyes, evidence of sleepless nights and the relentless pursuit of justice. The lines on my face seemed deeper, etched with the weight of the world I carried.

Turning on the tap, I splashed cold water on my face, hoping to jolt myself back to reality. Instead, the chilling droplets only served as a reminder of the chilling nature of the case that consumed me. The water trickled down my skin, mingling with the invisible tears that welled up within me. As I stumbled back to my bedroom, I glanced at the large board on the wall, filled with photographs, witness statements, and crime scene sketches. The board had become a collage of horrors. Each face, each piece of evidence, reminded me of my failures—of the justice I had yet to deliver.

I dressed my shaking body, still in shock, placing my shoes onto my blistered feet from walking home after the case. Everything reminded me of it, and how my life would never be normal again. I took a deep breath, my mind still entangled in the webs of the investigation.

The world outside seemed distant, muffled by the overwhelming noise inside my head. The weight of the unresolved case clung to me like an oppressive fog, making it difficult to think of anything else.

Leaving my apartment, I stepped out into the bustling city streets. The screams of car horns and distant chatter faded into the background as my mind continued to replay the details of the crime scene. I longed for a moment of respite, a break from the relentless grip the case had on me. It was a constant battle against evil, a relentless pursuit of justice that came at a cost. As I made my way to the station, I knew the weight of the young girl's murder would continue to haunt me, until the day I could finally bring her killer to justice—and find some semblance of peace for her, her family, and myself.

CHAPTER 6
DISGUISES

I waved my hand slowly, my mind still in another place for what seemed like weeks. I smiled when I saw a young man in a black taxi stop beside me, greeting me with a warm smile and bright blue eyes. I sighed in relief as I realised, I wouldn't be late to work—for once. I walked up to the musty, tinted window to show him where I was going, but as he rolled it down, he looked me up and down, as if I were fascinating to him. I started to get a weird feeling when I glanced over at what seemed to be a navigator in his lap. It read, "You have reached your destination." I shivered, knowing this man knew my address and had been expecting me to be here, waiting for a cab to get to work.

This was a planned operation, and I had fallen right into it with open eyes.

He kept staring at me, and trying to break the awkward silence, I asked him to place my bag in the boot of the car. He paused but then opened the door. I startled when he stepped out. What had seemed like a young athletic man, was actually a tall, muscular, middle-aged man with the build of a boxer. I gulped.

He bent down to pick up my large duffel bag and walked over to the boot of the taxi. My heart pounded, and my thoughts raced. I had no idea what was happening—or what would happen next.

He came back around the car and stood very close to me, his broad body almost touching mine. Abruptly, he swung the door open and stretched out his arm, gesturing for me to get inside.

I looked at the car door, leading into what I knew was certain death, and then looked back into his striking blue eyes. He must have noticed my hesitation because, before I could decide, he grabbed my arm and hastily pressed a .44 Magnum handgun to my neck, which was now violently pulsing with fear.

He whispered into my ear, "Get into the bag, or I will slice open every vein, every blood vessel, every measly organ inside your weak bag of bones of a body." Before me was a jet-black body bag, covered head to toe in what seemed to be flesh and chunky blood mixed with slime and sludge from previous victims no doubt.

That's when I knew I was in serious trouble.

My heart pounded in my chest as I frantically scanned the street, searching for anyone who might help, but what had been a busy main street had suddenly become as quiet as a secluded corner of a forgotten pathway. My seated heart pounded against my ribs when he pressed the gun harder against my neck, and I could feel my veins being pushed aside as he aimed to terrify me even more.

Reluctantly, I stepped into the backseat, tears streaming down my face, every bone in my body shaking profusely. He knelt down, and the rusted zip of the bag—obviously opened and closed many times before—was pulled open once again. I felt the need to vomit from the putrid smell and the bloodstains in the bag, but I knew it could cost me my life.

I crawled into the bag, relieved to see the small slits of makeshift air holes. I turned over with my back to the floor, staring up at him as he smiled, zipped me shut without hesitation, and slammed the car door closed. I felt completely defeated and helpless.

Once he had thrown me into the back seat, I peered through the makeshift holes and noticed the vehicle was old, its worn-out seats covered in stains and dust. The pungent smell of stale cigarettes and musty air filled the cramped space, making it difficult to breathe.

My heart started racing, and a sense of unease settled in when I realised the taxi had pulled away from the curb. I had no control over where the driver was taking me. Every turn the taxi made deepened my anxiety. The rhythmic creaking of the vehicle's suspension added a haunting soundtrack to my fear. I couldn't escape the relentless thought that I might be headed toward my own death.

The driver's silence throughout the journey only amplified my trepidation. There were no words exchanged, no reassurances to calm my racing thoughts. Instead, an eerie silence filled the air, broken only by the occasional crackling of the radio, playing some distorted tune. With each passing moment, my imagination ran wild with terrifying scenarios of what awaited me at the end of this unsettling ride. The shadows cast by the streetlights outside seemed to twist and contort, feeding my paranoia.

At last, the taxi came to a halt and my heart began to race. Quietly, he opened his door, and I took a deep breath, thinking I would get to see the sun again, to take a clean breath of air—but I was wrong. I heard him open the door, bending down as if to unzip the horror of the body bag, but he didn't. Instead, he grabbed the bag by the end, dragging it out of the car and throwing my barely breathing body onto the ground. Then he picked me up again, and I realised this sick monster was holding my weak body like a duffel bag. My dignity had been completely stripped away.

He kept walking for what felt like hours. My mind was traumatised—blaming myself for being so careless while also trying to plan an escape. At the same time, I wondered how anyone was ever going to find me.

I stopped to take a deep breath and acknowledged that my thoughts were racing—but then I realised I was having a panic attack.

Gasping for air, panic gripped me, and soon I felt the desperate need for oxygen surging through my veins, overwhelming my senses. Each inhale became a hurried gasp, the stale air filling my lungs with an unsettling heaviness. My breaths grew shallower but louder. Time became distorted, with seconds feeling like eternities as I battled the urge to let go and stare into the endless abyss forever. My heart pounded within my chest, an unsteady drumbeat of fear. I felt like I was dying, and all the oxygen left in my shaky body was rapidly slipping away. Beads of sweat dotted my forehead, my body drenched in a cold sheen of terror.

My limbs tensed and tingled as if I was losing feeling in them, mere accessories to my fearful body as oxygen became scarce. Dizziness consumed my consciousness, and my limbs weakened. I was terrified, crying floods of tears with no idea how to help myself. The edges of my vision blurred, swirling in a hazy dance of disorientation. I was as still as a lifeless body, yet my breathing wouldn't slow. Every time I willed myself to take a deep breath, nausea gnawed at my stomach—a sickening reminder of my dire situation.

With each passing second, my body grew weaker, my grip on reality slipping away. As my eyelids grew heavy, I could tell my face felt groggy and lifeless. I couldn't speak, couldn't move, couldn't even hear anything. All I could feel was my right arm shaking faster and faster and faster. I desperately grabbed onto it with my other hand but soon fell back into a wide stare and succumbed to the inevitable, surrendering to the black void that awaited me.

My mind was calm now—time didn't exist, and I couldn't feel anything, but my vision was fuzzy, and then he appeared. Suddenly, all the memories came flooding back.

CHAPTER 7
THE SAD REALITY

Moments, hours, or perhaps an eternity later, my senses began to stir. Like a flickering candle, awareness slowly rekindled within me. As my eyes fluttered open, the harsh reality quickly returned. My hands and feet still tingled. It felt like seeing the world for the first time, only it wasn't my world—it was a dark, empty warehouse that smelled of mould and cigarette smoke.

I gasped, realising I wasn't enclosed in that revolting bag anymore. Fresh air filled my lungs, I didn't care about the cigarette remanence or the gas, instead I savoured every moment. My eyes darted around, desperate for any sign of companionship, but the only thing in sight was what looked like a freezer a few meters away. My body tried to edge forward, but I came to the realisation I was tied to a chair, my wrists and ankles bleeding profusely from the restraints.

All I could do was sit and wait. Feeling around the chair, I noticed its cold metal features, and suddenly, my limbs grew weak and immobilized with fear. This was no ordinary chair—it was electric. I felt my heart leap into my throat; I was now petrified.

The dimly lit warehouse echoed with eerie silence, broken only by the distant sound of dripping water. Fear gripped me as I struggled against my bonds, the cold metal biting into my skin. Shadows danced on the walls, heightening my sense of dread, and the only sound I could hear was my own rapid breathing—shallow and desperate. Every creak and groan of the building sent shivers down my spine, amplifying my terror. The unknown loomed over me, filling my mind with horrific scenarios.

I wondered if I'd ever see my loved ones again, if I'd ever escape this nightmare.

Time felt like an eternity as I sat there, my mind oscillating between sheer panic and desperate hope. I strained my senses, attempting to detect any signs of movement or rescue, but in this desolate warehouse, it seemed I was utterly alone.

What truly drove me mad was the fact that I had no idea how long I'd been unconscious or how long it would take the detectives to realise something had happened to me. I had to cling to the tiny sliver of hope that someone would come for me, but how would they, when even I didn't know where I was?

My eyelids began to grow heavy, flickering as I struggled to stay awake. Just when I felt myself slipping into a restless sleep, I heard a voice—it wasn't close, but I could make out the words: "I have her, boss. What would you like me to do?" Then, silence.

A chill ran through my body, and my blood turned cold. This wasn't a random attack. They had specifically wanted *me*.

My mind spiralled into confusion, questioning why they'd targeted me. Why was I the one? Why was I in this chair? My thoughts raced uncontrollably, and I couldn't handle it anymore. In a desperate attempt for answers, I shouted, "What do you want with me? Please let me go! I have a family. I've met the love of my life and never got to tell him. Please don't do this!" I waited, my whole-body trembling.

Of course, I didn't have any close family, and the man I mentioned was just a friend—only I wished he wasn't.

Michael

That's his name, he cares about me in a way no-one else ever has and at that moment I realised that sitting here I wasn't even worried about myself, but rather the idea that I will never get to tell him I love him, or that he is the only person who has ever understood me. It wasn't exactly love at first sight but it was something like that. The first time we spoke, or the first time we laughed or the first Chinese we ordered into the office when a case got too difficult to go home, I felt it. An ache. Like a little electric burn. I felt my life change because of him. The second our eyes met. I knew I he would have a special mark in my life but I looked away because I was so sure I was just another girl to him.

But this monster didn't need to know that, and right now, I needed all the sympathy I could get.

Suddenly, I heard footsteps. They were loud and getting closer. My heart raced as I tried to make out who or what was coming. I felt my heart stop when I saw a huge black boot graze the curtains across from me.

In that moment, I froze. He knew I had recognised him—the beast who murdered that girl. The same distinctive black boots covered in mud, the tall and broad-shouldered figure—they could've been twins. He greeted me with a devilish smile, then took a sharp knife out of his pocket. I flinched but tried to stay calm, not wanting to show weakness.

"You will do what I say when I say it," he muttered, his voice as cold as his demeanour. "You will only speak when I tell you to. You will eat and drink when I tell you to. You know what happens if you don't. I'm sure you saw the work of my brother."

He made a small smirk and whispered, "It wasn't a murder-suicide, simply a disappointment." His words sent a shiver down my spine.

Then he walked across the room to a small, isolated fridge. I prayed it was for food or water, hoping with everything I had left, but it wasn't. As soon as he opened the door, the most pungent smell filled the room. He picked something up with a long, cruel smile and waved it in the air as if to show it to me. I squinted, struggling to make out what it was. Then I noticed something shiny in a rectangular shape on top of it. As I stared closer, the realisation hit me like a wave of nausea—it was a finger.

A finger.

Covered in ice and frozen blood. I knew I'd never forget that sight.

His monstrous feet slowly walked toward my trembling body, and I felt paralyzed, unable to speak. He leaned in close, his dirty, scarred face inches from mine. Tears welled up in my eyes as he whispered in a soft French accent, "I will rip every bone from your body and smile as your blood pools on the ground while your beautiful dark eyes shut forever."

I gulped and tried to hold myself together as he walked back to the fridge, placing the frozen finger back into the ice-cold compartment.

I felt so helpless, knowing I was a detective caught in a hostage situation, unsure of how to escape. I knew my best chance was finding a phone, but I was still trapped in that sharp metal chair, the cold steel digging into my back and thighs.

I was losing hope.

I had lost my spark.

My fight.

CHAPTER 8
ETERNAL DARKNESS

I knew I would be gone soon, and there was nothing I could do about it. My muscles started to ache, and I felt the weight of exhaustion settling into my bones. My mind was racing with thoughts of escape, but the restraints around my wrists and ankles kept me firmly in place. I couldn't even breathe freely or move my hand to scratch an itch. I realised how much we take for granted when we are free—until we're trapped and realise that we can't actually do anything except sit, look around, and think about all the things we could be doing or want to do. Losing my ability to control my body and actions made me feel so hopeless and weak almost immediately.

It was quite clear to me that getting out of here was most likely impossible, but I was determined. I knew that it wasn't just my life weighing down my shoulders; it was the lives of everyone else who had been taken and murdered, their cases forgotten or put on hold, while no one looked deeper. For all the people who didn't have families or anyone to fight for them, their cases were ignored. I've always hated people who look the other way. I then realised how much of a difference a detective could make, and I knew that I wanted to keep making that huge difference. So, I promised myself I had to keep my life and my job—I had to escape.

Suddenly, I caught faint murmurs of conversation drifting toward me from afar.

I strained my ears to listen, hoping to catch any clue that could aid my escape. The voices grew louder, and my senses sharpened in anticipation. Fear and adrenaline surged through my veins, as if preparing me for what lay ahead. Without a second thought, I mustered all the strength within me to push myself up from the metal chair. I pushed and pushed. I could feel the metal cutting into me slowly, digging into my now dry and pale skin, but it was almost done. Then, as a result of the tremendous force I was placing on it, the chair groaned and creaked under my weight, as if protesting my defiance. The restraints strained against the force I was now using, threatening to keep me imprisoned.

As I finally broke the rigid metal clasps open, the sound of my escape echoed in the stillness of the room. Panic set in as I realised that he must have heard me. My survival instinct kicked in, urging me to run for my life. I bolted toward the nearest exit, my heart pounding in my chest like a drum. The distant voices grew louder and louder, now filled with urgency and anger, realising my escape. Every step I took now felt like my life depended on it, but my hope was short-lived as I watched two tall figures emerge from the sly shadows, their menacing forms blocking my path. Fear gripped me tightly, restricting my breath and paralysing my muscles.

I tried to fight back, to resist their grasp, but their huge silhouettes crushed what was left of me. Their grip was like steel around my arms. Their voices cut through the air like a chilling wind, filled with hatred and pain as my captor knelt down to tower over my small body to say, "This is what happens when you detectives get too involved." A cruel smile danced on his lips. The words hung in the air as I felt a cold dread settle in the pit of my stomach, knowing what awaited me.

I glimpsed a minuscule moment of hesitation in their eyes before darkness enveloped them, and their eyes that once glistened became a devilish matte black.

In that tragic moment, I realised they would stop at nothing to protect their secrets, even if it meant taking a life. My life. One of them knelt down just enough to look me in the eyes and quickly placed a knife across my throat. Even as he watched the tears form in my bloodshot eyes and my nostrils scrunch up in agony and pain, he kept pushing on my neck as if he had no emotion. He was completely dead inside. Soon enough, I could feel the blood drip down onto my chest that no longer rose up and down to inhale and exhale. As he recklessly pressed the knife down further, my consciousness began to fade away, knowing this was the end for me. I couldn't help but wonder how many others had met the same fate in the same pursuit of justice as mine.

The echoes of their psychopathic voices and devilish laughs became my last moments. I felt empty and abandoned, but still guilty, knowing I left that girl's family with no justice—the justice I had promised her family, her parents, the justice I had promised her. The innocent, beautiful young teenage girl who had just gotten caught up in all this, exactly like I had. She never got justice.

Alexandra.

And now my death was going to go down exactly like hers—with no way to trace it. Detectives completely confused and no evidence. I had always been at peace with death, but not when it came to these men. Because I knew that something would happen after my eyes were never to open again—whether it was a drastic betrayal, a suicide, a murder, or even the impossible chance of help finding me. Only I wouldn't be there—just my lifeless corpse would be left. Suddenly, I wasn't so at peace with death anymore. Still, it was over now. I took a small gasp, savouring every tiny millisecond, and my eyelids became so heavy. In that moment, my eyes shut, and my last sight was the blood-splattered ceiling staring down at me.

Or what was left of me.

CHAPTER 9
GONE WITHOUT A TRACE

It was 10:55. She had never been this late to work before, and I was starting to worry. Yes, she was usually late, but not quite this late. I started to think maybe she was in trouble as I peered down at my phone and saw no message or text from her. Everyone in the office took a small glance at her empty seat, and each of them displayed a face showing their confusion and concern. We were being assigned to a case I knew she would love to be part of, and it broke my heart that she wasn't here to witness it. I tried to stay focused and put together a reason why she wouldn't show up to work on a normal Tuesday morning.

Chief Superintendent Hope Reynolds slowly walked into the room, avoiding eye contact with anyone. She quietly closed the door shut with a heavy slam, and all eyes immediately turned to look at her as she walked up to the front of the room. The silence was deafening until she opened her mouth gently and, speaking barely above a whisper, said, "I am so sorry to inform you all of the death of a well-known and adored detective who most of you will have known for many years. It brings me great sadness to tell you that Detective Nancy Richmond's body was discovered earlier this morning in an abandoned parking lot with a knife in the palm of her hand. The police initially thought to rule it as a suicide, but it has since been determined this is false. Due to several strands of DNA on the knife, as well as the position of the sever going straight through the back of the neck, which is extremely uncommon in suicide cases. Therefore, this is now an ongoing homicide investigation. Any of you may get as involved or remain separate from the case as you wish. However, due to the fact that she was a friend and colleague to many of you, I am giving you all the rest of the day off to clear your minds and prepare to return to work tomorrow."

At that moment, my heart felt numb, knowing she wasn't just late to work—she would never be coming back. I didn't get to say goodbye. She was gone. My heart was beating out of my chest, and my whole body felt shaky, but the feeling didn't last long as rage consumed me, along with a desperate need to find the monster who took the life of my best friend and partner. That fateful morning, I left the precinct earlier than usual, unable to bear the weight of my grief and anger any longer. The rage within me surged like a tempest, threatening to consume my every thought. We had been inseparable, partners in crime-solving and in life. Our bond transcended the badge; it was a deep, unbreakable connection that had sustained us through countless cases. Now, she was gone, taken from me in such a cruel and heartless manner.

In the days that followed, my obsession with solving her murder consumed me entirely. I locked myself away in my dimly lit, cluttered office, surrounded by a sea of case files and crime scene photographs. I pored over every detail, every potential lead, searching for any clue that might bring her killer to justice. It was during one particularly gruelling late-night session that I stumbled upon a breakthrough. Buried within the chaotic jumble of evidence, I discovered a connection that sent a shiver down my spine. The night before her murder, her driver had been brutally slain, his throat slit. The police had ruled it as a careless murder with intent to steal the car since his taxi was stolen and still hadn't been recovered. It was a grim puzzle piece that finally began to fit. I then realised that the murderer hadn't targeted her by chance; they had deliberately chosen her as the next victim, planning it days before, all while she remained oblivious to the danger lurking in the shadows.

Determined to unearth the truth, I set out to untangle the web of deception that had engulfed her, vowing to avenge her untimely demise and bring her killer to justice—knowing now that he could be considered a serial killer on the run.

The first place I knew I had to go was the police station. With a newfound determination coursing through my veins, I bolted from my cluttered office, my heart pounding in my chest. The scent of rain hung heavy in the air as I rushed to my car, fumbling for my keys with trembling hands. Every second counted, and I couldn't afford to lose any more time. The police station loomed ahead, and as I ventured inside, I scoured through records and documents, my fingers dancing across keyboards as I unearthed fragments of information. It was then that a peculiar detail emerged: the stolen taxi had been traced back to a small, nondescript taxi station on the outskirts of town.

Leaving the police station behind, I raced to this seemingly unremarkable taxi hub. It was a dimly lit place, a patchwork of flickering fluorescent lights and the distant hum of radios. The dispatcher, a grizzled man with a world-weary expression, provided me with a key piece of information. On the night of her murder, a cab had been dispatched to her location. This was my first concrete link to the murderer's path. My mind whirred with possibilities as I left the station, a cacophony of thoughts and questions swirling like a tempest in my mind.

Returning home, the late hours cast long shadows across my study, where walls were adorned with crime scene photos and maps. Determination merged with confusion as I sifted through the abundance of evidence, a jigsaw puzzle with pieces that refused to fit together. Frustration gnawed at me, but I wouldn't be defeated. I laid out a large sheet of paper, and with coloured markers, I began to craft a sprawling mind map, connecting the disparate threads of information. As the night wore on, clarity gradually emerged from the chaos. The killer's pattern began to reveal itself in intricate detail, leading me down a chilling path that would ultimately unmask the shadowy figure responsible for Nancy's murder.

It had now become obvious to me that this serial killer was the same person who had murdered the taxi driver, Nancy, and Alexandra, but their motive was unexplainable. There was nothing in common among the victims, all killed in different ways, but each had their throat slit and left no evidence to follow. This made me realise the case was deeper than the others. This wasn't just a hit-and-run or revenge for a past fight. This was a planned operation, carefully formed, leaving no evidence behind, gaining something the police were unaware of.

I shivered when I saw that there had been three murders in three days, which meant there was an extremely high chance of another murder on the fourth day. I had one night to figure out what was happening behind the scenes. As the night continued its relentless march, I became increasingly entangled in the intricate web of this investigation. Each scrap of evidence presented itself as a convoluted puzzle piece, eagerly beckoning me to decipher its mysteries. The stark, unforgiving light from the desk lamp cast elongated shadows across the walls of my small, dimly lit study. The room felt like a world suspended in time, trapped within the embrace of this complex case.

Amid the chaos of my investigation, stacks of case files and an assortment of crime scene photographs lay strewn across the surface of my desk, as if my workspace had become a battleground. Each document was a soldier in the relentless war for truth. The scattered papers told the story of my sleepless nights and tireless efforts, a testament to my unwavering commitment to unravelling the disaster before me.

My pursuit of justice was not merely a job; it was an all-encompassing obsession. With every tick of the clock, the mysteries deepened, and the weight of the unsolved crime pressed ever more heavily upon my shoulders. Yet, in the solitude of my study, bathed in the cold glow of the desk lamp, I persevered, knowing that somewhere amidst the chaos of evidence and shadows, the answers I sought lay waiting to be discovered.

With each passing hour, the tension in the room grew, and my temples began to throb in protest. My eyes, bloodshot and weary, scanned over the intricate notes and photographs. I could feel a persistent headache taking root at the base of my skull, but there was no respite in sight. The relentless drive to bring the killer to justice pushed me beyond the boundaries of exhaustion. As the clock struck the darkest hours of the night, I reached for my phone, my fingers trembling with fatigue. I dialled the number of Detective Ericka O, my trusted colleague and the only person I felt I could turn to after the death of my love.

Ericka was known for her razor-sharp intellect and unwavering commitment to the truth. The phone rang, and after what seemed like an eternity, Ericka's voice crackled through the line. We exchanged weary greetings, our voices weighted with the grief and determination we shared. With a mutual understanding, we agreed to meet at my office to delve further into the case.

Hours passed in a haze of conversation, analysis, and determination. Eventually, we methodically pieced together the puzzle. It became clear that all the individuals connected to the case had one common thread: a woman named Nicole Stark. She was a spectre in the shadows—a beautiful young woman with long, dirty blonde hair and striking facial features that masked the darkness within.

Nicole Stark was not just a pretty face; she was an intelligence powerhouse, rumoured to have been hiding in plain sight for years. Her ability to manipulate even the most hardened criminals was legendary. She had inherited her mastery of the criminal world from her father, a notorious mastermind who had wielded influence over countless lives through the dark web. Serving 16 life sentences without parole, he was a formidable, dangerous figure who had left a legacy of crime in his wake. As the first rays of dawn crept through my window, fatigue had long since taken its toll on our bodies, but a newfound resolve had taken root in our hearts. Together, we had unravelled the threads of the conspiracy, exposing Nicole Stark as the hidden puppeteer orchestrating the chaos. The true depth of her influence remained a chilling feeling, but we knew that our pursuit of justice had just taken a strong turn into the dangerous world she controlled.

After an exhaustive night of investigation, we knew we needed to take our findings to the next level. As the morning sun rose, casting hopeful rays of light through the blinds of my study, we decided to take our discoveries to the police station. The precinct bustled with activity as officers went about their duties. We walked through the familiar corridors, heading straight for the office of our superior, Chief Superintendent Hope Reynolds. She was known for her unwavering dedication to solving the toughest cases and had a reputation for having a sixth sense when it came to identifying key leads.

As we entered her office, Chief Reynolds looked up from her paperwork, her sharp eyes appraising us. She had a presence that commanded respect, and she didn't waste words. We quickly recounted the developments in the case, presenting the evidence that tied everything back to Nicole Stark, the elusive mastermind. Hope listened intently, her expression giving nothing away. When we finished, she leaned back in her chair, steepling her fingers in thought. "This is serious," she finally said, her voice low and measured. "If Nicole Stark is behind all of this, we're dealing with a level of criminal sophistication we haven't seen in years."

With a decisive nod, Hope picked up the phone and issued orders to mobilize a task force to apprehend Nicole Stark. Ericka and I were both placed at the forefront of the investigation, given the responsibility to track down and bring to justice the woman who had managed to manipulate the criminal underworld from the shadows for so long. As we left Hope's office, we both sighed in relief, knowing we had done all we could, but we felt a renewed sense of determination. The stakes were higher than ever, but we were no longer alone in our pursuit of justice. With the full resources of the police department behind us, we set out to unmask Nicole Stark and dismantle the criminal empire she had inherited from her notorious father. It was a battle that would test our skills, our resolve, and our commitment to the truth.

CHAPTER 10

ALWAYS ONE STEP AHEAD

My name is Nicole Stark. I've always been a master of this game. In the criminal underworld, where power shifts like quicksand, I've learned to glide through the treacherous waters with unparalleled finesse. Ever since I stepped into my father's dark legacy, I've held onto one unwavering truth: to survive, you must always be one step ahead.

I've always felt invisible in my penthouse, hidden away from the prying eyes of the world below. The city sprawls beneath me, a chaotic community I have manipulated from behind the scenes for as long as I can remember. My long blond hair falls in waves around me, framing a face that exudes the deceptive allure of beauty. With my striking facial features, I've had grown men wrapped around my finger, and I've never hesitated to use that to my advantage.

My eyes, however, tell a different story. Behind their piercing blue gaze lies the intellect of a chess grandmaster—always analysing, always plotting. My father, a criminal mastermind, ruled lives through the dark web, and I had been his most attentive pupil. His legacy is my domain, and I am its reigning boss. Yet, I have created my own legacy—my daughter, Alexandra. She almost took the fall for a crime she didn't commit, though somehow her DNA was the only evidence left at the scene. She was my everything, which is why I took her out of my world. I wanted to give her the chance to have a life with friends and fun—a childhood I never got to experience. I gave her the opportunity to live whichever life she wanted, under a new identity, but now she was getting too close, and someone chose to do something about it.

In the corridors of power, the mere whisper of my name sends shivers down the spines of those who dare to defy me. Yet, beneath the facade of allure and charm, I harbour a darker side, one I guard with ruthless determination. It's this duality—this ability to wear masks—that has kept me hidden for so long, always one step ahead of those who seek to unveil my secrets.

As I survey the city below, I know my empire is under threat. Detectives Michael Harrison and Ericka Occomore are closing in, driven by an unwavering pursuit of justice. Still, I'm not one to cower in the face of danger. I relish the challenge, for in the shadows of deception, I am the master of my own destiny. In the silence of my secluded penthouse, where the world's chaos feels like a distant whisper, I contemplate the trail of destruction left in my wake. My thoughts linger on the dark secrets buried beneath layers of deceit and death—secrets that stretch back over the years.

The city has always been my canvas. Every person who has killed someone, done time, or even those remotely dangerous—they are all wrapped around my little finger. I relish the sense of freedom knowing I am never afraid because I hold the power. And when you have power over people, you have power over the place. From the shadows, I have orchestrated the demise of countless souls, using my influence to ensure their silence. Their voices are but echoes, lost to the unforgiving night, their secrets buried in unmarked graves. To the world outside, they were mere statistics in the relentless pursuit of a serial killer.

I allowed myself a sly smile, savouring the exquisite irony. The police, led by Detectives Michael Harrison and Ericka Occomore, are indeed on the lookout for a serial killer. Little do they know they are hunting the very architect of the carnage they seek to end. As I contemplated my own brilliance, a sense of invincibility washed over me. The detectives are skilled, no doubt, but I am the maestro in the symphony of deception.

They are chasing shadows, while I manipulate every move from my throne of obscurity. The world believes me to be a beautiful enigma, a woman of mystery, but none suspect the extent of my malevolent genius.

With each passing day, I revel in the thrill of the hunt. The detectives, like bloodhounds on a twisted trail, remain oblivious to the puppeteer behind the curtain. They are clever, perhaps the cleverest I've ever faced, but I am always one step ahead. As they struggle to piece together the fragmented puzzle, I continue to pull the strings. My mastery of the dark arts ensures I remain the orchestrator of chaos, hidden in plain sight. I have always been followed closely by the police, but never this close—not until I had to send men to murder witnesses because they were getting too close. Yet, I don't doubt for a second that everything will work out just as it always does.

To them, my mind is a well-oiled machine churning with strategies and contingencies. Every move I make is calculated, every loose end swiftly tied. I revel in the knowledge that, while they chase shadows, I craft nightmares. The city is my canvas, and I paint its darkest corners with strokes of terror—each stroke a testament to my cunning. Yet, even as I celebrate my mastery of deception, a nagging doubt lingers. An inkling that, perhaps—just perhaps—there are factors beyond even my control. A flicker of concern ignites in my consciousness, like a match in a room filled with gasoline. I dismiss it as paranoia, but in the darkest recesses of my mind, a haunting whisper persists, warning me that the detectives are edging ever closer to the truth.

Days turn into restless nights, and still nothing—just story after story on the news about every murder, every hitman I've sent out. Oh, how euphoric it feels to play God. I watch as my empire of darkness tips the mountain of their discoveries. The detectives' relentless pursuit—their unwavering commitment to justice—is a formidable adversary. I have danced on the edge of the abyss for too long, and now, I can feel its cold breath on my neck.

Yet, my resolve remains unshaken. In the intricate game of cat and mouse we play, I am determined to stay the course. The strategy that got me this far will ensure, as it always does, that I remain one step ahead.

CHAPTER 11
THE CHASE - MICHAEL

The air in the precinct hung heavy with the weight of our pursuit. We were in the heart of a chase unlike any we had ever encountered. The city's darkness seemed more oppressive, its secrets more elusive, as we delved deeper into the shadows, determined to unmask the serial killer lurking within. With every passing day, our investigation bore fruit. Threads of evidence, once desperate and confusing, began weaving a sinister tapestry that pointed to a hidden malevolence. It was an unbelievably complex puzzle, except one where the pieces were stained with the blood of the poor or the innocent.

As I repeatedly examined the evidence board in our makeshift war room, the faces of the victims stared back at me, their eyes pleading for justice. Each crime scene photograph told a story of horror and despair, a testament to the brutality of this monster, but it was also a trail, a twisted path that we were determined to follow to its bitter end. Ericka, with her uncanny ability to spot connections where others saw chaos, was relentless in her pursuit of leads. She pored over the victim profiles, cross-referencing details, searching for any hint of a pattern.

Her dedication was unwavering, her intellect a beacon of hope in the darkest of times.

Together, we dissected the evidence, tracing the killer's footsteps through a city gripped by fear. The more we uncovered, the clearer the image became: our serial killer was cunning and methodical, leaving no trace that could easily be followed. It was as though they had been schooled in the art of murder, their every move calculated to confound and mislead.

Yet, we are detectives, and the chase was our calling. We followed the leads, tirelessly interviewed witnesses, and left no stone unturned. Each night, as I lay in my bed, the puzzle pieces swirled in my mind, dancing on the edge of understanding. There were moments when it felt like the killer was toying with us, taunting us with their cleverly concealed tracks.

I knew one thing for certain: the chase was far from over. With each day that passed, we got closer to unravelling the twisted riddle that had gripped our city in terror. The serial killer might be a shadow in the night, but we are detectives, and our determination burned brighter than the darkest abyss. Justice was our solemn promise, and we would not rest until the truth was laid bare and the killer was brought to justice.

As I sifted through the stack of dusty old documents, each one bearing the weight of years gone by, I stumbled upon a revelation that sent a chill down my spine. Nicole

Stark, the elusive serial killer we had been chasing, had a past as twisted and dark as her present. It was a story that began in a broken home, a tale of innocence stolen and a descent into darkness that was as inevitable as it was heart breaking. Nicole's childhood was far from idyllic. She was raised in a family shattered by violence and dysfunction. Her father, a man whose name I can't help but shudder at, was a volatile and abusive figure. He had a darkness within him, a monstrous side that manifested itself in unspeakable acts of cruelty. It was he who had killed Nicole's mother in a fit of rage, leaving behind a shattered family in his wake.

As the documents slowly revealed themselves, Nicole's life took a nightmarish turn from that moment forward. After her mother's murder, her father vanished into the night, leaving his traumatised daughter to bounce from one foster home to another, but she was not one to be contained. At the tender age of fifteen, she ran away from one such foster home, and from that moment on, she vanished from the system, leaving no trace.

It's a haunting revelation that unravels the enigma that is Nicole Stark. Her disappearance from the foster system was a calculated move, one that allowed her to escape the confines of a troubled past and disappear into the underworld, where she would go on to master the art of deception and manipulation. It's as though she erased her identity, leaving no breadcrumbs for anyone to follow. As I delved deeper into the documents, I couldn't help but wonder what drove her to become the person she is today. The scars of her stolen childhood, the memories of her mother's murder, and the abandonment by her father must have shaped her in ways we can't begin to fathom. It's also clear that the darkness that resides within her was always there, waiting for the right moment to emerge.

Nicole Stark is not just a serial killer. She's a product of a twisted and tormented past, a survivor who has become the embodiment of the nightmares that once haunted her. And as the pieces of her tragic story fell into place, I couldn't help but feel that we were closer than ever to understanding the mind of the monster we were chasing.

The realisation of Nicole Stark's stolen childhood and her traumatic past sent shivers down our spines. Detective Ericka and I had been focused on uncovering her motives as a serial killer, but now we had stumbled upon a far more sinister truth: Nicole was a fugitive, a criminal with a history that was as haunting as it was extensive.

As we scrutinized her records, it became evident that Nicole had been arrested multiple times in the past, her charges ranging from petty theft to assault. However, what sent an ice-cold wave of fear through us was the fact that she had managed to break out of prison, not once, but several times. It was as though she possessed an uncanny ability to slip through the cracks of the justice system, disappearing into the shadows each time.

I couldn't help but think of all the times we had been close to catching her, only for her to elude us time and time again. It was a chilling realisation that we had been dealing with a fugitive, a woman who had perfected the art of vanishing, leaving no trail for us to follow. Ericka and I exchanged uneasy glances as the gravity of our discovery sank in. The question that gnawed at the back of our minds was, "What else had Nicole Stark managed to keep hidden?" Her ability to evade capture was a testament to her cunning and resourcefulness, and it left us with an unsettling feeling that we had barely scratched the surface of her secrets.

The fear that gripped us was not just about solving a case anymore. It was about facing an adversary who had operated with impunity for years, a woman who had lived in the shadows, evading justice, and leaving a trail of victims in her wake. We were not just dealing with a serial killer; we were dealing with a fugitive who had outsmarted us at every turn.

As we continued to sift through Nicole's records, the room seemed to close in around us, the weight of our pursuit pressing down like a suffocating darkness. The hunt for Nicole Stark had taken a chilling turn, and we were left with a sense of foreboding, realising that the most dangerous game we had ever played was far from over.

The once warm sun that grazed my cheeks had now switched to a burst of brightness, disturbing the sleep I so desperately needed. When a smile would have normally crept across my face in anticipation of the day ahead, I was now reminded that the woman whose beautiful smile lit up my face was gone, dying with no one by her side, knowing that her body may never be found. With the guilt of letting her down, I rolled back over and allowed my frown to consume me. My eyes became heavy, and suddenly, I was not motivated to open them anymore. I realised now that this was going to be harder than I anticipated, but using every ounce of unspoken love I had for her, I squinted, opening my eyes only slightly and threw myself out of the bed encasing me from fulfilling the only thing keeping me sane—finding the monster who took her from this world.

From me.

CHAPTER 12
THE FAÇADE

It was time. The day I had been dreading since the day she died: the funeral. The day that anyone and everyone could come and pay their respects, whether they had ever spoken to her or not. The whole thing was absurd. Seeing her worst enemies or the most jealous people she had ever met, all dressed in black and pretending to care, was maddening. I couldn't help but wonder if this unbelievable monster of a human was crazy enough to turn up to such an event. The atmosphere was so heavy with grief, and my heart sank as I approached the venue, a looming sense of finality hanging in the air. The skies seemed to mirror the sombre mood, draped in heavy clouds that threatened to release their burden at any moment. I couldn't escape the reality that this event marked the end of an era, the closing chapter of a life that had touched so many, especially mine.

As I entered the funeral hall, the subdued murmur of conversations and the occasional sniffle filled the space. The room was adorned with flowers, their vibrant colours clashing with the pervasive melancholy. People from different walks of life gathered, each with their own stories and memories of her. It was a peculiar sight to witness the juxtaposition of genuine mourners and those who attended merely for appearances or attention, surrounding a person who had made my life whole.

I found myself standing in front of her casket, a stark reminder of the irreversible nature of mortality. Memories flooded my mind—moments together that could never be forgotten, endless laughter, and tears we had shared. The contrast between the life encapsulated in those memories and the stillness of the present was overwhelming.

Amidst the sea of mourners, I couldn't help but notice a young female figure standing alone in the corner, seemingly detached from the collective sorrow. It was the same enigmatic individual whose presence I had doubted earlier. There was an air of mystery about her, and I couldn't shake the feeling that she harboured secrets related to her—secrets that I hadn't yet uncovered. The thought made my blood run cold—the idea that this stranger knew more about the way the love of my life had been taken from me than I did.

As the eulogies began, each speaker painted a vivid portrait of her. Stories unfolded like chapters of a novel, revealing facets of her personality that many were unaware of, except me. It became evident that, despite the complexities and contradictions, she had left an indelible mark on those who had crossed paths with her, even for a moment. The funeral procession moved outside, and the rain, which had held back until now, began to fall. It felt as though the heavens themselves were mourning, tears cascading down like a collective expression of sorrow. The sound of raindrops on umbrellas and the rustle of leaves merged with the subdued whispers of farewell.

As we laid her to rest, the gravity of the moment weighed heavily on my shoulders. The finality of the act hit me like a tidal wave, and I couldn't escape the realisation that life, with all its uncertainties and complexities, was fleeting. The cemetery became a silent witness to the passage of time, a repository of stories that would endure in the hearts of those left behind.

In the aftermath of the funeral, as people dispersed and the echoes of mourning faded, a profound sense of emptiness and isolation settled in. The challenge of navigating a world without her became my new reality. The days ahead promised a journey of healing, reflection, and the gradual acceptance of a void that I knew could never be fully filled.

The rain persisted as I left the cemetery, scared that I would fall into a hole too deep for me to drag myself out of. Each drop was a poignant reminder of the tears shed not only by the heavens but by those who had bid their final farewells. The journey home was solemn, the rhythmic patter of rain on the car roof providing a melancholic soundtrack to my thoughts. As I navigated through the wet streets, my mind was consumed by a relentless curiosity about the mysterious figure from the funeral.

Arriving home, I couldn't shake the feeling that there was more to the story than met the eye. The events of the day had left me with a lingering sense of unease, a suspicion that the funeral was not just a gathering of mourners but a stage for hidden agendas. I needed answers. I delved into the task of investigating the enigmatic person who had stood apart from the crowd. A nameless face in a sea of grieving faces, yet there was an aura of significance surrounding her. My computer became a portal to a world of secrets as I scoured social media, news articles, and public records, hoping to unearth any connections or clues that would shed light on her identity.

Hours turned into late-night solitude as I pieced together fragments of information. The mysterious individual seemed to have a knack for staying off the radar, their digital footprint minimal. However, persistence paid off as I stumbled upon a thread linking her to a web of clandestine dealings and covert connections. It was a revelation that left me both intrigued and apprehensive.

Driven by a sense of duty, justice, and an insatiable need to understand the truth, I expanded my investigation. The secrets I uncovered painted a portrait of Nicole as a complex and multifaceted individual. Her life had been a tapestry woven with threads of intrigue, hidden alliances, and a trail of unresolved mysteries.

In the days that followed, I found myself navigating a labyrinth of deception and half-truths. It was slowly driving me insane, but after nearly losing my mind, it became apparent that the funeral was not merely a gathering of mourners but a convergence of individuals with vested interests, each holding a piece of the puzzle. The more I delved into the shadows, the more questions arose, creating a tapestry of uncertainty that mirrored a complexity in her I had never seen before.

As I continued my investigation, alliances shifted, and allegiances were tested. I treaded cautiously, mindful of the thin line between revelation and danger. The journey of discovery became a personal odyssey, a quest for closure and justice. The secrets that unfolded were not confined to the realm of the departed but extended into the lives of those left behind. It was a revelation that blurred the lines between right and wrong, morality and necessity, leaving me standing at the crossroads of a moral dilemma.

In the shadows of the investigation, I grappled with the realisation that some truths were better left buried. Yet, the relentless pursuit of justice compelled me to press forward, unravelling the layers of deception that shrouded the legacy of a woman whose life was as enigmatic as the secrets she took to her grave. It seemed that everything and everyone was in my way.

CHAPTER 13
TOYING WITH INSANITY

I sat alone in my dimly lit office that smelled of food I had ordered weeks ago and the sweat that had left my body days before. Yet, it was my comfort place, even though I was always surrounded by the haunting echoes of unsolved cases that lined the shelves. The city outside carried on with its daily hustle, oblivious to the storm brewing within me. Frustration gnawed at my insides—a hunger fuelled by the case slipping through my fingers.

The walls of the precinct seemed to close in as I pored over the files, each piece of evidence leading me down a path of false hope. The anger, a simmering rage that had driven me, now threatened to consume me. The case was on the brink of going cold, and I felt the weight of impending failure pressing down on me.

Every lead turned out to be a dead end, every witness statement a mirage. I couldn't trust anyone—not the witnesses, not my colleagues, not even my own instincts. This new sense of distrust was tearing me apart from the inside out. The frustration twisted my perception, turning allies into potential conspirators.

Days blurred into nights as I revisited crime scenes, scrutinized evidence, and interrogated suspects. The city that once felt familiar now seemed like a treacherous labyrinth of deceit. I was trapped at its centre, grappling with the suffocating realisation that time was slipping away.

My sleep was becoming elusive, my mind haunted by the faces of the victims and the shadows of the unknown perpetrator. The anger that had fuelled my determination now threatened to consume me. I couldn't escape the nagging suspicion that the very people I relied on—colleagues, witnesses, even the police—might be part of the intricate web of deception.

Paranoia clawed at my mind as I questioned every motive and every alibi. The once-clear line between truth and falsehood blurred, and I found myself second-guessing every piece of information that had once seemed reliable. The anger that had ignited my pursuit of justice now turned inward, a self-destructive force eroding my confidence. Late one night, drowning in my thoughts, I stared at a wall covered in photographs and notes. The faces of the victims stared back at me, accusing me of failure. I slammed my fist against the corkboard, the sound echoing through the empty room.

"I won't let this case go cold," I muttered, realising the desperation in my voice was a haunting echo.

In the solitude of my office, I faced the demons that lurked within my mind. The weight of the unsolved case pressed upon me like a vice, squeezing the last seeds of reason from my consciousness. I questioned every decision, replaying conversations and analysing evidence until reality itself became a distorted puzzle.

The city outside continued its relentless pace, oblivious to the internal storm raging inside of me. My descent into madness mirrored the chaos of the investigation, and the line between perpetrator and investigator blurred as I spiralled.

As the case threatened to slip away from me, I stood at the precipice of my own unravelling. The anger that had fuelled my pursuit of justice had transformed into a volatile force, threatening to consume me whole. The city's cold indifference mirrored my struggle, and, teetering on the edge of sanity, I faced a choice—succumb to the abyss or claw my way back to sanity for a chancc to play this right. No case had ever been like this before—it was physically breaking me from the inside out. I knew it wouldn't be easy, but I didn't think it would make me question my sanity or whom I could trust. This case was different from the others. It was deeper.

I had to go back to work today, but no one looked at me as they had before. No one knew what to say or how to act, knowing what I had been going through with her case and death. The silence became deafening, but it was then broken by Chief Superintendent Reynolds, who came to tell us our duties for the day. I knew I needed this to bring back the small sense of normality I had left, but she left me until last to assign work. She slowly said I had no work. I didn't want her pity, but I felt like maybe I needed it.

CHAPTER 14

OUT OF TIME

I sat in my office, tense and focused. The case I'd been working on for months meant everything to me. Every lead followed, every witness interviewed, all to bring justice to the victim. However, as my boss called us all in for a meeting, dread filled the air. Everyone knew a meeting in the middle of the day was never a good thing—the last time we had an abrupt meeting, it was because of her death. As Chief Superintendent Reynolds pursed her lips, all eyes dropped, and suddenly, everyone turned to me. Each person seemed unsure of what to say or do—it was as if she had died all over again.

The case had gone cold.

My heart pounded in my chest like a relentless drumbeat, each thud echoing through the hollow cavern of my ribs. The air in the room felt thick, suffocating, as Hope delivered the news that shattered my world in an instant. Anger surged through my veins like molten lava, searing every fibre of my being. My fists clenched so tightly that my knuckles turned white, the pressure of my grip almost suffocating.

This couldn't be happening.

Not now, not when I'd poured every ounce of my being into this case. Every lead meticulously followed, every dead end exhaustively explored, all in pursuit of justice for her—a justice no one else seemed to care about. I'd been so close, the tantalizing promise of a breakthrough dangling just within reach like a shimmering mirage in the desert. And now, the last grain of hope I had held onto so desperately had vanished.

A surge of frustration and despair threatened to consume me, a tidal wave of emotions crashing against the fragile dam of my composure. How could this happen?

How could the threads of my painstakingly constructed case unravel so effortlessly, slipping through my fingers like grains of sand? I felt as if I were drowning in a sea of incompetence and injustice, the weight of failure pressing down on me, leaving me with only the thought of her death, and no one left to avenge her. I had never felt a heavier guilt weighing on me.

Amidst the storm raging within me, a single ember of determination flickered to life—a stubborn refusal to surrender to defeat. I may have been dealt a devastating blow, but I refused to let it break me. If anything, it only fuelled the fire burning within me, igniting a fierce determination to see this through to the bitter end.

So, with a deep breath to steady my trembling limbs, I squared my shoulders and met Hope's gaze with steely determination. I could tell she didn't want to deliver the news; I could see it in her eyes. It looked as if she was feeling the same cloud of guilt slowly settling over her. The battle may have been lost, but the war was far from over.

And as long as my heart was still beating, I would fight on, relentless in my pursuit of showing Nancy that someone cared enough to keep going. If no one else, I cared.

Without a word, I stormed out of the meeting room. I had never fully understood what it meant for your mind to race, but now I got it. My mind felt as if it was overflowing—each thought another wave, maliciously placed to push me over the edge. Walking through the desperate drops of rain soaking me, I placed my feet slowly one in front of the other, finding it difficult to keep myself balanced upright. I was so distraught it was as if nothing else mattered. I just wanted to leave.

I headed to my car, barely able to see through my now streaming eyes, hands trembling as I fumbled with the keys. The strength I had been holding my fists together with had now evaporated. Once inside, I couldn't contain the torrent of emotions anymore. Tears streamed down my face as I pounded my fist against the steering wheel. The thing I wanted more than anything, the thing that had seemed to give me a purpose after she died, was taken from me in an instant. With just three words, my whole world fell apart.

In a haze of fury and despair, I gripped the steering wheel with an intensity I didn't even know I was capable of, my foot pressing down on the accelerator with reckless abandon born of desperation. The world outside blurred into a terrifying montage of colours and shapes, the lines of the highway stretching out before me like a twisted ribbon of fate. Tears streamed down my cheeks unchecked, their salty sting mingling with the bitter taste of defeat that still lingered on my tongue.

Thoughts of the case, of the victim, consumed me like a vicious fire, burning away every last drop of reason and restraint. Their faces flickered before my mind's eye, haunting spectres that danced on the edge of my consciousness, their silent accusations a damning indictment of my failure. I had promised them justice, promised her justice, sworn to see their tormentors brought to account, and yet here I was, powerless to fulfil that sacred oath.

The weight of my own inadequacy pressed down upon me, suffocating me with its relentless embrace. How could I have been so blind, so naïve, to believe that I alone could stem the tide of injustice that threatened to engulf us all? It was a fool's errand, a task doomed to end in futility and despair.

The harsh reality dawned on me just before I had time to react. A blaring horn and screeching tires brought me back to the present. I glanced up, my vision swimming with unshed tears, to see a massive truck careening toward me, its headlights blazing like twin beacons of impending doom. Panic surged through my veins like a tidal wave, paralyzing me with its icy grip, as I realised with a sickening jolt that I had strayed into its path.

Darkness.

Time seemed to slow to a crawl as the truck bore down upon me. I tried to swerve, to evade the oncoming fate, but it was too late. The impact, when it came, was deafening in its ferocity—a cacophony of twisted metal and shattering glass that reverberated through every bone in my body.

My world exploded into a riot of pain and chaos as the car was tossed like a child's toy in the grip of some malevolent giant, the force of the collision sending shockwaves rippling through every fibre of my being. I was thrown against the seat with bone-jarring force, my breath knocked from my lungs in a gut-wrenching gasp as the airbag exploded into being with a thunderous roar.

And then, as suddenly as it had begun, the chaos subsided, leaving behind a hushed silence, broken only by the sound of my ragged breathing and the distant wail of sirens. I sat there, dazed and disoriented, blood trickling from a gash on my forehead as I struggled to make sense of the devastation that surrounded me. I tried to keep breathing, but I truly didn't know if I still wanted to. I had nothing left.

CHAPTER 15
FATE OR LUCK

Amidst the wreckage and ruin, a single thought burned like a beacon of hope in the encroaching darkness: I was still alive.

Despite the odds, despite the overwhelming despair that threatened to engulf me, I had survived. And as long as there was breath in my body and fire in my soul, I began to see that I would continue to fight on. Not only out of human instinct but for myself and for the many things I had left to live for.

Undaunted by the trials and tribulations ahead, unwavering in my quest for redemption and retribution.

CHAPTER 16
ONE LAST TRY

Light, but not a normal sort of light—the kind everyone squints at when they first see it, the kind you can't turn on at night because it's simply too bright. Hospital lights.

As I peered through my eyelashes, once covered in dried-up blood, I dared to open my eyes. I had underestimated how heavy my eyelids had become. It felt like I hadn't opened them in months, but it had only been hours. It felt so draining to open my eyes, only to see no one—no emergency contact, no family or friends. It reminded me of how completely alone I was.

Before I had time to dwell in my sorrows, I was quickly bombarded by a swarm of questions. The sound of machines beeping rhythmically in the background punctuated the eerie silence. A rush of panic surged through me as I tried to piece together what had happened.

Moments later, a group of doctors entered the room, their faces grave with concern. They explained that I had been in a car crash, but the unsettling part was that I had no recollection of it whatsoever. It was as if a curtain had been drawn over my memory, leaving me stranded in a fog of confusion. As they probed further, asking questions about my identity, I struggled to provide coherent answers.

It was then that they realised something was terribly wrong—I had no idea who I was.

My mind was a blank canvas, devoid of any personal history or memories. Fear gnawed at the edges of my consciousness as I grappled with this newfound reality. Who was I? Where did I come from? Questions swirled in my mind, unanswered and haunting. The doctors exchanged concerned glances, their expressions mirroring my own growing sense of dread. In that moment, I felt utterly lost, adrift in a sea of uncertainty with no lifeline to cling to.

Days blurred into nights as the doctors conducted a battery of tests, each one more exhaustive than the last. I became a mere subject—poked and prodded, hooked up to machines that beeped incessantly, measuring every heartbeat and breath. Loneliness crept in like a shadow, enveloping me in its cold embrace. There were no familiar faces, no comforting voices to anchor me to the world I had lost.

I longed for someone to talk to, someone who could shed light on the darkness that engulfed me, but the sterile walls of the hospital offered no solace, no respite from the relentless march of time. With each passing day, I grew weary of the tests, the endless stream of doctors and nurses who examined me with clinical detachment. I yearned for escape, for a fleeting moment of reprieve from the suffocating monotony of my existence.

As the days turned into weeks and the sun rose and set outside the hospital window, a sense of anticipation began to permeate the air whenever the group of doctors entered my room.

Their footsteps seemed to echo with purpose as they approached my bedside, their expressions a mixture of determination and concern. They would gather around me, a cluster of white coats and stethoscopes, poring over my medical charts with intense focus. Their discussions were animated, punctuated by the occasional nod or furrowed brow as they delved deeper into the enigma that was my condition.

Each test brought with it a new wave of hope and trepidation, as we waited with bated breath for the results that held the key to unlocking the mystery of my lost memories. I could see the determination etched on their faces, a silent promise that they would not rest until they had pieced together the puzzle of my fractured identity.

They described the symptoms in painstaking detail, dissecting every nuance of my cognitive functions and neurological responses. They spoke of fragmented memories and elusive recollections, of a mind trapped in a labyrinth of confusion and uncertainty.

With each passing examination, their excitement seemed to mount, like explorers on the brink of a discovery that would redefine the boundaries of human understanding. They poured over brain scans and MRI images, searching for clues amidst the tangled web of neurons and synapses that formed the landscape of my mind. And then, after what felt like an eternity of waiting, they delivered their diagnosis with a solemnity that reverberated through the room. They spoke of a condition that had eluded them for so long, a condition that lay at the heart of my confusion. I watched intensely as their lips parted, desperate to know what I had suffered for so long, hoping for an end to all the white coats and questions.

"PTCS," they whispered, the string of letters hanging in the air like a weighty confession.

It was four simple letters, yet it carried with it the weight of a thousand unanswered questions, a thousand fractured memories waiting to be rediscovered.

“Post traumatic confusional state, a rare form of amnesia”. In that moment, as the truth washed over me like a wave crashing against the shore, I felt a strange sense of relief. For though my memories may have been lost to the depths of my subconscious, I was no longer adrift in a sea of uncertainty. I had a name for the darkness that had consumed me, a name that held the promise of a path forward—a path toward reclaiming the fragments of my lost identity.

CHAPTER 17

ROCK BOTTOM

The next day arrived like a reluctant guest, its arrival marked not by the gentle embrace of dawn's first light but by the persistent hum of machinery and the plastic scent that permeated the hospital room. I stirred from a fitful slumber; my body weighed down by the heaviness of another day confined within these sterile walls.

As I gradually reclaimed my hold on my senses, I found myself grappling with a sense of disorientation that lingered like a thick fog, obscuring the boundaries between dream and reality. My limbs felt leaden, as if anchored to the hospital bed by invisible chains forged from the weight of my own uncertainty.

With a weary sigh, I let my gaze drift around the room, taking in the clinical white walls and the array of medical equipment that loomed ominously in the corners like silent sentinels guarding over my restless sleep. The rhythm of the machines—their steady beeping and whirring—served as a constant reminder of the fragile balance between life and death that hung in the air like a palpable presence.

I hated this place with a severe intensity that bordered on irrationality. I despised every sterile surface and antiseptic scent that assaulted my senses with each passing moment. It was a prison of sorts, a place where time seemed to stand still, trapping me in a perpetual state of emptiness with no clear path forward.

And yet, despite my strong desire to escape, I knew deep down that I was powerless to change my circumstances. This hospital room had become my new reality, a bleak landscape populated by faceless strangers who moved about with purposeful intent, their voices a distant murmur echoing off the walls like the ghostly remnants of a forgotten dream.

I longed for the outside world, for the warmth of the sun on my skin and the gentle rustle of leaves in the breeze. However, here within the confines of these sterile walls, such simple pleasures were just distant memories, fading into obscurity with each passing day.

And so, I resigned myself to another day spent in this desolate purgatory, counting the minutes until the next round of tests and treatments would begin anew. It was a routine that had become all too familiar—a monotonous cycle of waiting and wondering.

With a languid stretch, I roused myself from the depths of sleep, each movement accompanied by the symphony of creaking joints and protesting muscles. The transition from the realm of dreams to the harsh reality of the hospital room was a gradual one, like emerging from the depths of a murky pond into the blinding light of day.

As my senses slowly sharpened, I became acutely aware of the various sensations around me. The persistent rhythmic beeping of machines echoed in the stillness, a constant metronome that measured the passage of time with unwavering precision. Outside the window, the world carried on with its relentless march, oblivious to the struggles that consumed me. I could hear the muffled sounds of life filtering through the glass—the distant hum of traffic, the faint chirping of birds—reminders of the vibrant world that lay just beyond my reach.

Here, within the confines of this hospital room, time seemed to stand still, trapped in a perpetual state of suspended animation. Each day bled seamlessly into the next, a monotonous blur of routine and repetition that offered little respite from the suffocating sense of isolation that gnawed at the edges of my consciousness.

I hated this place with every fibre of my being, hated the way it seemed to swallow me whole, leaving me feeling small and insignificant in its vast, impersonal embrace.

And yet, I knew deep down that I was powerless to escape, bound by invisible chains forged from the weight of my own uncertainty.

CHAPTER 18

IF HOPE WAS A PERSON

I lay there in my hospital bed, surrounded by the same white walls and the constant hum of medical equipment. It was all getting too repetitive, and it felt like my mind was slipping away from me. It had been months since the car crash that stole away my memories, leaving me trapped in this place, disconnected from my past and uncertain of my future.

Then he walked in—I had no clue who he was, but he was the first person in months to look at me like I wasn't just an unfortunate patient who had no idea who he was. He looked at me like he knew things about me that I didn't, like he knew me before... before the accident. His presence was like a beacon of hope in the sea of uncertainty that had become my life. I couldn't recall a single moment we might have shared before this, but there was something about him that felt familiar—and something about me that seemed very familiar to him. Maybe it was the kindness in his eyes or the way his voice carried a sense of reassurance.

He spoke to me, his words cutting through the fog of confusion clouding my mind. "Hey there," he said, his voice soft yet filled with determination. "It's me, Marcus. I know you might not remember me, Michael, but I'm here to help you."

I nodded slowly, trying to grasp the fleeting fragments of memory that danced just beyond my reach, but there was nothing—just an empty void where my past should have been. Still, a sense of trust welled up inside me as I looked into Marcus's eyes. Somehow, instinctively, I knew he was someone I could rely on.

He told me about the accident, about the tireless effort he had put into unravelling the mystery of who I was and how I ended up here. He promised to be my caretaker, to guide me through the darkness until I found my way back to myself. And in that moment, I knew I wasn't alone in this journey.

CHAPTER 19
QUESTIONS

Days turned into weeks, and I only seemed to be getting worse. Everything I knew when I went to sleep seemed to vanish when I awoke every morning. It seemed that the person I called Marcus was different. I could feel the brink of insanity preparing to swallow me whole. I was exhausted every time I woke up. I had no recollection of where I was or who was actually Marcus, because every day, he was different.

Every morning, a new house, a new person looking after me, but all with the same name—Marcus.

As the days passed, my memories slowly but surely returned, but my confusion every morning still caused me to question if I was truly remembering or just felt like I was. I couldn't shake the nagging feeling that something wasn't right. It was as if, with every step forward I took in rediscovering my past, I was simultaneously being pulled further away from reality. It felt like for every memory I regained, I got further from what I knew to be real. It was like trying to put together a puzzle where the pieces kept changing shape.

Every memory brought up a flood of emotions—happiness, sadness, love, and regret, but they were all mixed up and confusing, like a jumbled mess in my mind. I couldn't tell what was true anymore. I started questioning not only Marcus but also the amount of power he had over me and how he had full control over which medications I took and how often. I began to feel so lost that I couldn't trust anyone. The medications they gave me were supposed to help, but I soon realised I felt like they were making things worse. Not only did I take them every morning, but also at night, and I passed out almost immediately after. I then put together that this was most likely not how this medication was supposed to work, or if what Marcus was giving me was even actually the medication I was prescribed. It was as if they were pulling me away from reality instead of helping me find it. The medications seemed to only cloud my mind even more, and I started to wonder if they were really meant to help me or if they were keeping me trapped in this hazy limbo.

So, one night, fuelled by suspicion and desperation, I made the decision not to take them.

At night, when everything was quiet and Marcus came upstairs to give me my medication, I watched and waited until the second the door closed to spit it out. I started coughing violently as it was such a large pill, but I came to realise later on that I was still awake much later than on any other day. I sat up in my bed, staring ahead of me when I heard footsteps. Checking the time, it was exactly 3 a.m. Almost as if this had been planned to happen, I quickly turned off my light and jumped into bed, now knowing the medication I had been taking was most likely sleeping pills, and it all started making sense.

I watched from the shadows of my room as a tall figure entered, broad-shouldered with long dirty blonde hair. Even peeking out of one eye, I could see it was Marcus. My whole body turned ice-cold, and I found myself unable to move. Every muscle in my body shook, and my mind was overwhelmed with questions—none prepared to wait their turn. It was a sea of emotions, each wave a tear closer to darting out of my eye in fear.

I was petrified but also confused, and I was sure there was an explanation. However, my mind froze when he viciously threw off my bed cover. I lay so still, while my body and mind were screaming. I was absolutely petrified, but before I could take a breath to think, he threw up both of my arms and placed my legs together. I lay completely limp, giving him full control over my body as he wrapped his now huge, icy hands around my arms and legs and hoisted me over his back. The world spun around me as I struggled to make sense of what was happening. It felt as though my heart had stopped beating. As time continued to trickle by, I found myself caught in a whirlwind of conflicting emotions. His once reassuring presence now felt ominous, terrifying, and unknown, casting a shadow of doubt over the fragile semblance of reality I had clung to.

I watched in petrified silence as he left me exposed and vulnerable to the cold grip of fear that wrapped itself around my heart. My mind screamed for me to move, to fight back, but my body remained frozen in place, paralyzed by the overwhelming sense of dread that coursed through my veins—his touch sending a shiver down my spine.

As he carried me down the staircase, each step seemed to blur into the next in a tsunami of chaos and confusion. The world around me spun dizzily, disorienting me further with every movement.

The flickering lights above cast eerie shadows that danced along the walls, their shapes morphing and twisting into grotesque forms that seemed to taunt me from the darkness. The sound of our footsteps echoed through the empty corridors, reverberating like a haunting.

CHAPTER 20
THE LIES UNFOLD

With every descent, I felt as though I was being dragged deeper into a nightmare from which there was no escape. The air grew thick with a sense of foreboding, a tangible weight that pressed down upon me like a suffocating blanket, leaving me gasping for breath.

My mind whirled with a cacophony of thoughts and emotions, each one crashing over me like a relentless tide, threatening to pull me under into the depths of despair. It was as though the very fabric of my reality was unravelling before my eyes, leaving me stranded in a world that bore so little resemblance to the one I once knew.

Amidst the chaos, a profound sense of disorientation washed over me like a tidal wave, leaving me grasping for a lifeline in the swirling sea of confusion. It was a dizzying sensation, like being caught in the eye of a storm, where every direction seemed equally fraught with peril.

As we reached the bottom of the staircase, my senses reeled from the sudden upheaval of my reality. The world around me seemed to tilt and sway, the ground shifting beneath my feet as though I stood on unsteady ground. It was a harrowing descent into the unknown, a journey that plunged me deeper into the abyss of uncertainty with every passing moment.

Marcus's grip tightened around me as we reached the bottom of the staircase, his intentions shrouded in mystery. I couldn't help but wonder what awaited me in the darkness below, what secrets lay hidden in the shadows that danced along the walls.

As he carried me further into the unknown, I couldn't shake the feeling that I was being led down a path from which there was no return, a path that would forever alter the course of my life—or even end it.

After what felt like hours in the car, we stopped, but it wasn't a normal stop; it was abrupt, jolting the car forward. I held back any sign that I was conscious, swallowing harshly as Marcus got out. When he left me in the car, I realised something was terribly wrong. Out of all the places I had guessed we might be going; this was not even close. It was a barbershop. Marcus had driven into the darkness of the night at 3 a.m. and brought me with him, unconscious, to get his hair done? My confusion only grew, but I knew there was something deeper happening.

I lifted my chin just enough to stare out of the tinted window, catching a slight view of Marcus pulling out a large sum of money to pay for a haircut. The barber counted every last note. As Marcus started to exit the barbershop, I frantically forced myself back into the limp position I held before. When he got back into the car, I could barely recognise him. With jet-black hair, a freshly cut beard, and glasses, he was almost unrecognisable. It was as if when I woke up tomorrow, his once familiar features would now be unrecognisable, forcing me to believe I had simply forgotten what he looked like.

At that moment, the dots started aligning—but in a way that sent a shiver down my spine and made my blood run cold. I now saw that this was much deeper than I could have ever imagined. The man I called a friend was only here to make me feel like I was going insane.

My heart raced as the pieces of the puzzle began to fall into place. Each step was a journey into the depths of my mind, a landscape fraught with fragments of the past waiting to be unearthed. Memories, like elusive whispers, danced at the edges of my consciousness—teasingly evasive yet tantalizingly close. It was a delicate dance between truth and illusion, a narrative woven by the threads of my subconscious and the whispered doubts planted by Marcus.

His words echoed in the chambers of my mind, sowing seeds of uncertainty amidst the fertile soil of remembrance. Was I truly remembering, or merely constructing a facade of coherence amidst the chaos of forgotten moments?

Marcus, with his penetrating gaze and persuasive demeanour, sought to ensnare me within the confines of his narrative. To him, I was a puzzle to be solved, a riddle to be deciphered within the limits of his own creation. He wielded the power of suggestion like a master craftsman, sculpting my perceptions with deft precision, moulding them into shapes that suited his agenda.

Yet, amidst the fog of doubt that threatened to engulf me, there remained a flicker of defiance—a stubborn refusal to succumb to the shadows of uncertainty. Deep within the recesses of my being, there burned an ember of resilience, a steadfast belief in the validity of my own experiences.

And so, as I stood at the crossroads of memory and manipulation, I made a choice. I chose to trust in the whispers of my own heart, to embrace the fragments of remembrance that fluttered like delicate butterflies within the garden of my mind. For although Marcus may seek to cast doubt upon the veracity of my recollections, he could never extinguish the flame of truth that burned within me.

I had been remembering things all along, but Marcus wanted me to think I was losing my mind, that I was still trapped in the depths of amnesia. The realisation hit me like a freight train, filling me with a mix of anger, blind rage, and fear. I had no idea what to do or how to act, but I knew I had to play along and not let Marcus know I had discovered his little secret.

My only question was: why? Why was he going through all this money, time, and effort to make me feel insane? As I started thinking about it, I realised this was a major endeavour—he had to wake up every day and tell me I had forgotten, then drug me, change his identity, and take us to a new location. My mind raced, and tears began to form. Someone with this level of dedication was part of something big, and somehow, I had gotten myself into it. There was absolutely nothing I could do about it. As I stared at Marcus, realising how much of a monster he truly was and how close I had been to him—he had almost become family but had lied to my face the entire time—I felt rage building inside me. It became unbearable.

I noticed a gun in the passenger seat, staring me in the eye.

With each passing moment, I could feel my rage building, fuelled by the burning desire to reclaim my life and confront the demons lurking in the shadows. As I remembered the gun, I knew that no matter what was going on, there would be a place and time to find out the full story or exact revenge—and that time was not now. I would never stop fighting to reclaim the truth that had been stolen from me.

Now, there was a blackness about my eyes whenever I dared to think about his face. I feared the thought of having to look him in the eyes again, not knowing if I would be able to hold myself back from tearing him to shreds. As the realisation settled in, a cold wave of betrayal washed over me, chilling me to the bone. Marcus, the person I had trusted implicitly, had been weaving a web of lies and deceit around me all this time. The thought coiled itself into the crevices of my brain, threatening to consume me whole. How could someone I held so dear turn out to be the architect of my torment?

In the darkness of my mind, his face emerged, twisted into a sinister grin that mocked my naivety. Every word he had ever spoken echoed with a hollow ring of falsehood. The memories we shared seemed tainted, stained with the poison of his deception. I felt like a fool, played like a puppet in his cruel game.

Shrouding my thoughts in a suffocating haze of disbelief and rage, I thought about the fear of even being in the same vicinity as him again. The mere idea of confronting him filled me with primal dread, a sensation that crawled beneath my skin like a thousand tiny spiders.

In my dreams, his presence haunted me, a spectre of treachery that lurked in the shadows of my subconscious. I would find myself trapped in a labyrinth of twisted corridors, pursued relentlessly by his malevolent gaze. Each time I turned a corner, he was there, his eyes gleaming with malice as he revelled in my despair.

The anticipation of facing him again was a heavy burden, weighing down on my soul with unbearable weight. I could feel the tendrils of anxiety tightening around my chest, constricting my breath until it felt like I was suffocating. The prospect of masking my emotions, of feigning composure in his presence, seemed like an insurmountable challenge.

Yet, amidst the turmoil of my emotions, there lingered a sliver of determination. I refused to be cowed by his deceit, to let him dictate the course of my life. Somewhere deep within me, a flicker of defiance burned brightly, fuelling my resolve to confront him and reclaim my sense of self. However, until that moment came, I would continue to steel myself against the dread of facing him again, knowing that the battle ahead would not just be waged with fists, but with the strength of my spirit. I knew that keeping this game up was my only advantage before I found out more. So, I had to keep it to myself, no matter how difficult it was bound to be.

CHAPTER 21
THE GAMES BEGIN

He threw the door open, and I fell limp, forgetting that he could not become aware that I was conscious. I was shaking uncontrollably; every muscle in my body had lost control. I was petrified. Yet to him, all he saw was my lethargic body being dragged out of the back of the car.

I put everything I had into lying quietly, attempting not to raise his suspicion. My mind was beginning to breach the limits of sanity. Things like this didn't happen to people like me. I had my boring job and a simple life—until now. I was part of something bigger.

Suddenly, I felt my head bash against a door and realised we had approached the barbershop and gone in, but it was silent. No voices, no machines, not even a pin drop—it was completely empty, even though I had just witnessed him pay a hefty amount of money to a man who had seemed to disappear.

CHAPTER 22

WAS IT WORTH IT

Waking up with the sun had always been a comfort, the soft rays slipping through the blinds, gently coaxing me out of sleep, but today, something was wrong. There was no warm light, no familiar surroundings—just darkness and a foul, suffocating stench.

My mind was groggy, fighting through a fog of confusion as I tried to remember where I was and how I'd ended up here. Panic surged as it hit me—I didn't know. The realisation tightened around my chest like a vice.

Suddenly, the walls of the bag I had been transported in for so long seemed to close in, suffocating me. I wasn't supposed to be here; I was never supposed to end up in a place like this. My heart raced, a scream tearing through my throat as I thrashed, desperate to escape the nightmarish prison I'd woken up in.

Almost immediately after, I remembered everything—where I was, what was going on, and, most importantly, the tiny detail that may have cost me my life.

I had to keep quiet.

CHAPTER 23
THE MANOR – MICHAEL

I kept quiet for what felt like hours, or days, or minutes. I had lost all sense of time, and no light could project into the black duffle bag, which meant I had lost any sense of how many days or nights this had been going on—but that was about to change.

Footsteps walked up to me. I was lying in what seemed like a small room in complete darkness, but just as my heart beat with both fear and relief, I felt the zipper. The zipper that could only be opened from the outside—the zipper that had forced me to encase every word I said and count every breath I took. It was a prison—not just a literal one, but a prison of my mind.

The zipper moved painfully slowly, as if I were being teased or tested for consciousness. Reluctantly, I closed my eyes. I had to play it safe. I had no idea where I was or with whom. I was terrified and completely out of my depth, and there was nothing I could do but pretend it wasn't happening.

I took my last deep breath and let my eyelids weigh me down to a natural end of my awareness. The zipper fully opened. I felt the breeze of clean air flow over my face, and that was a feeling I would now cherish for the remainder of my life. I slowly felt two people silently grab my head and legs as they lifted me up. I fell limp, ensuring that every ounce of my body was completely floppy, making sure there was no way I could get caught.

They brought me to a chair and sat me upright. Every footstep sent another tremor through me, making me feel extremely vulnerable. I was now sitting upright when a hard hand slapped across my face harder than ever before. At that moment, I flinched and was forced to open my eyes—to a beautiful manor. The ceilings were full of artwork and angels. It was almost poetic that such a brutal act was taking place in this gorgeous building. The light was shining through the huge stained-glass windows. It was surreal—almost magical.

I took a deep breath of the clean air. It almost felt ethereal, as if I had been taking my first breath of life.

CHAPTER 24

THE MANOR – NICOLE

After all I had gone through for her, my daughter still had no justice—only the mistakes I had made and mysterious cars following me.

I had gotten nowhere.

The person I had loved the most in life was gone, and I couldn't do anything. She was my everything, my greatest achievement. Yes, I call myself a mastermind, but the three minutes I took walking to her house cost my child her life. I was drowning in guilt to the point that I went limp and allowed myself to be taken to this place.

I had nothing left.

The person I lived for was gone, and I would die knowing I couldn't find out who it was. I was ready to go. Suddenly, a voice came from what seemed to be a speaker in front of me, and it started speaking.

CHAPTER 25
THE MANOR – AMELIA

"My name is Amelia. I have taken and tortured you both because of what you did to me, for the life you gave me, for the person I am.

Nicole, I took your daughter from you with joy. I was on the other end of the phone that night. I am the reason the police won't stop chasing you. I am the reason you have that scar across your stomach that you have never told anyone about after you gave birth to your sweet Alexandra —or rather, that's what you think."

CHAPTER 26
THE MANOR – NICOLE

I could not have been more confused. I was sitting on a chair in a beautiful manor, being spoken to from behind closed doors through a voice modulator.

I was finished. I didn't have the energy or the fight left in me to go on. I just wanted to pass and be with my daughter.

However, as the words came out, my heart fluttered. This person knew she was my daughter—a fact I held close to my heart, known by no one except us, and the scar. The scar I'd had across my stomach from giving birth with complications I was never told about.

I passed out during her birth, and it had always been devastating to me, knowing I didn't hear my baby's first cry or know why my birth couldn't have been natural. Instead, I woke up in agony with a scar across my stomach that is still with me to this day. It was the most vulnerable part of me, and the fact that this person knew it made my heart shudder.

CHAPTER 27
THE MANOR – AMELIA

"Michael, I am the reason you lost her.

Your little sweetheart—she was in my way, but I never wanted her. I wanted you. She was the only thing standing in my way of getting to you. That's a little sad, isn't it? The only person in your life I had to get rid of to get to you was your silly little girlfriend, and, well, you know how that went.

I am the reason you had that crash; you see.

It is so easy to manipulate a person when they depend on you. Marcus was your rock, and I have now shown you how easy it is for your rock to hit you across the head without you realising.

I was that figure at the funeral and the one person who didn't come up during all those endless discussions and takeaway nights."

CHAPTER 28
THE MANOR – MICHAEL

I sat there with my eyes wide open like a child and glanced to my right to see another woman with those beautiful blue eyes and long blond hair that could have any man wrapped around her finger.

This was her. Nicole Stark.

Now nothing made sense. Every single word said was true, and only those I was close to would know that. That is why it pained me that they were right.

She was my everything, and taking her did, in fact, rip me apart. Although what hurt me more than her death was that we never got our chance or rather I didn't. My life was built on a solar system that spun around Nancy and that was something held close to my heart.

I felt completely victimised. I was an easy target.

CHAPTER 29
THE MANOR – AMELIA

I am the reason, and I'm here to tell you why. My name is Amelia, and I have never known my last name.

I have a piece of paper in my hand right now—a drop of Nicole's blood and Michael's blood, too—with a test. This piece of paper explains the life I've lived and why the lives of Nancy and Alexandra had to end. Marcus will now hand them to you.

Do those names look familiar to you? Surprise—they are yours. Crazy, isn't it? And you see that name at the top? That is my name. That is my birth certificate.

You are my birth parents. Hey, Mum and Dad—funny seeing you.

Nicole, when you woke up from giving birth, you had a caesarean. That is the reason for the scar along your stomach.

You had twin sisters, one of whom had to go, as your family knew that even one child could destroy our whole family legacy, let alone twins. A face the same, the same DNA—it could've destroyed everything: our placement of evidence or hiding from security cameras—nothing would work with two, but you yourself were a twin separated at birth from your brother, and it still haunts you to this day. The idea that your parents chose you over him, and he was dropped into the foster care system. Ironic, really—I was that sibling. Your father knew that since you always grieved the loss of your brother, you wouldn't have given one of us up and would have just run with us both for our entire lives, so he took me. Your father took me into the crime system. My own grandfather wanted to give me a life of suffering, running, death, and no sense of belonging, all because of her—Alexandra. She took any chance I had at a life, and you didn't even know.

Children really are punished for the sins of their parents.

I will come out now for you both to see the face of your daughter. I'm sure you're excited.

CHAPTER 30
THE MANOR – NICOLE

She took my breath away. My heart stopped beating for a second, and my mouth muttered, “Alexandra?”, but she was dead, and this was not my daughter.

She had beautiful eyes, but this girl had eyes like the devil and a smile almost like my own. She was exactly the same. I couldn’t stop staring—she had the same nose, the same face, the same hair, the same body, the same persona as she stared back at me not daring to look away.

Everything about the scar made sense.

She was completely and utterly right. Right about everything, I did pass out during labour and when I woke up I remember the way everyone was looking at me, as if they knew something I didn’t. I had thought all the quietly exchanged glances, the lack of eye contact, and the plastered-on smiles were just nerves—an unspoken reaction to the overwhelming fact that I still had to give up my beautiful baby. We had all accepted that. Only, something still felt undeniably off.

But I was exhausted, so delirious from the hours of labour and the emotional toll—that I ignored it, dismissing it as pure disbelief. Only now did I see that it wasn't any of the things I had assumed.

It was guilt.

When Alexandra was placed in my arms, I thought I would feel an immense love, a deep connection to her. But I didn't. I woke up feeling completely detached, as if something was missing—or rather, someone. She was missing. The girl standing before me now was my daughter. I knew Alexandra was, to my knowledge, my only child. Yet this girl—she could have been her relative, her lookalike, her sister.

Her **twin**.

"No child is born broken. They are broken by their experiences." – Dr. Gabor Mate

www.ingramcontent.com/pod-product-compliance
Lightning Source LLC
Chambersburg PA
CBHW070609310726
48982CB00001B/28

* 9 7 8 1 6 6 6 4 1 1 6 8 3 *